Fuddles
-and-
Puddles

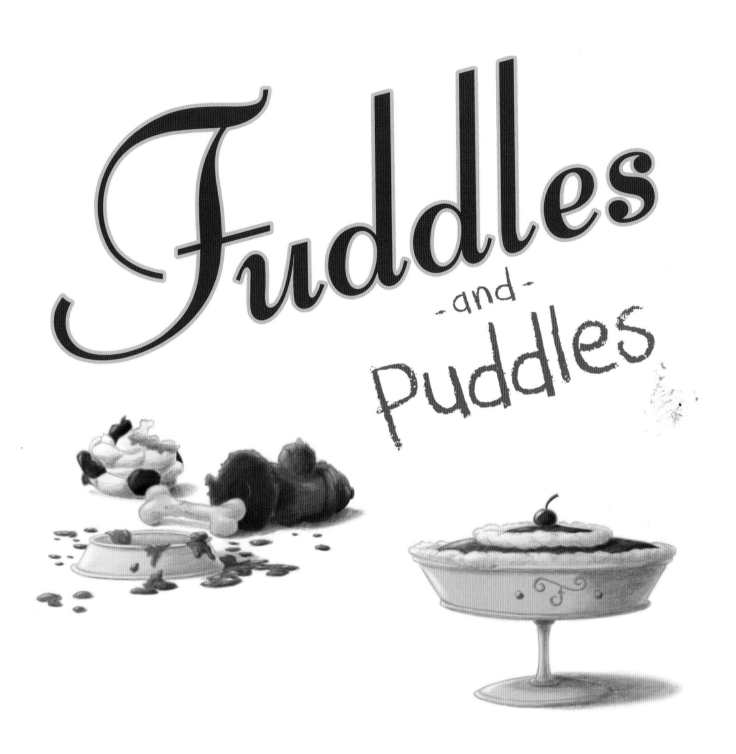

This book is dedicated to Fran Coleman,
my Cupertino High School art teacher, who challenged
me to open my eyes to the world of art.

• • •

I'd like to thank a father at a Fuddles book signing at
Vroman's Bookstore in Pasadena, California,
for suggesting the name Puddles.

ALADDIN

An imprint of Simon & Schuster Children's Publishing Division

1230 Avenue of the Americas, New York, NY 10020

First Aladdin hardcover edition September 2016

Copyright © 2016 by Frans Vischer

All rights reserved, including the right of reproduction in whole or in part in any form.

ALADDIN is a trademark of Simon & Schuster, Inc., and related logo is a registered trademark of Simon & Schuster, Inc.

For information about special discounts for bulk purchases, please contact Simon & Schuster Special Sales

at 1-866-506-1949 or business@simonandschuster.com.

The Simon & Schuster Speakers Bureau can bring authors to your live event. For more information or to book an event

contact the Simon & Schuster Speakers Bureau at 1-866-248-3049 or visit our website at www.simonspeakers.com.

Book designed by Karina Granda

The text of this book was set in Wade Sans Light.

The illustrations for this book were rendered digitally.

Manufactured in China 0716 SCP

2 4 6 8 10 9 7 5 3 1

Library of Congress Control Number 2015960463

ISBN 978-1-4814-3839-1 (hc)

ISBN 978-1-4814-3840-7 (eBook)

Fuddles
-and-
Puddles

WRITTEN AND ILLUSTRATED BY Frans Vischer

Aladdin
NEW YORK LONDON TORONTO SYDNEY NEW DELHI

Fuddles was a fat, pampered cat.

One afternoon, he was enjoying a tasty cat nap when he felt something wet and slobbery.

Me-ewww!

His delicious dream had turned into . . .

a nasty nightmare!

Fuddles woke up tired and troubled.

And now his tummy rumbled. Dinner called.

He went to the kitchen and gasped.

What was this? A puddle?

Puddle?!

Arf!
Arf!

Who let a drooling dog in the house?

"It's okay, Fuddles," said Mom. "You have a new friend."

Fuddles didn't want a new friend. Certainly not one that barked and slobbered and wet the floor!

"He's so cute and tiny," said one of the kids. "Let's call him Puddles."

Fuddles was so disgusted, he lost his appetite.

That night, Fuddles didn't sleep one wink.

That pest kept

whining, crying, and howling.

The next morning, and every morning after that,
wherever Fuddles went,

Puddles followed along.

Only when they were outside would
Fuddles—sometimes—get a break. Puddles

sniffed,

dug,

and chased,

while Fuddles

dozed,

stretched,

and dined.

One day, Fuddles was catching up
on his beauty sleep.

But as usual, Puddles had other ideas, like . . .

eating Fuddles's food. Fuddles had finally had enough!
"GET OUT OF HERE! THIS IS MY HOUSE."

Puddles yelped and ran away. After that, Puddles kept his
distance. Fuddles was delighted.

A few weeks later, Fuddles was happily sunning himself, when he spotted a yummy avocado. *What a nice before-dinner snack!*

He carefully climbed,

slowly but surely,

licking his lips,

but then . . .

He suddenly found himself *over* the fence,
on top of the dog next door's house.

Uh-oh, Fuddles worried. Was this his ninth and final life?!

He whined and cried and howled.

HELP! H-E-L-P!

The neighbor dog went back to his bone
while Puddles proudly stood guard,

and a shaky Fuddles climbed onto his back.

Safe and sound back in the yard,
Puddles gave Fuddles a great big lick.

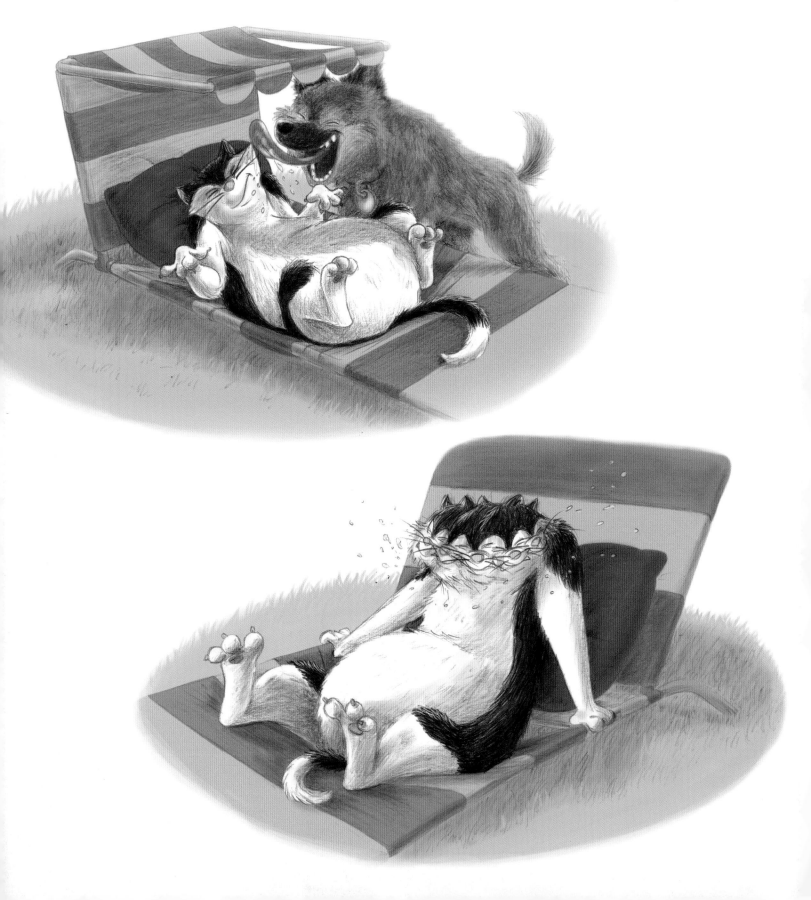

And Fuddles smiled!

Puddles had saved Fuddles's life!

Sure, he still licked and slobbered,

and barked and howled,

sniffed and jumped,

and chased Fuddles all over the house.

But now it was **their** house.